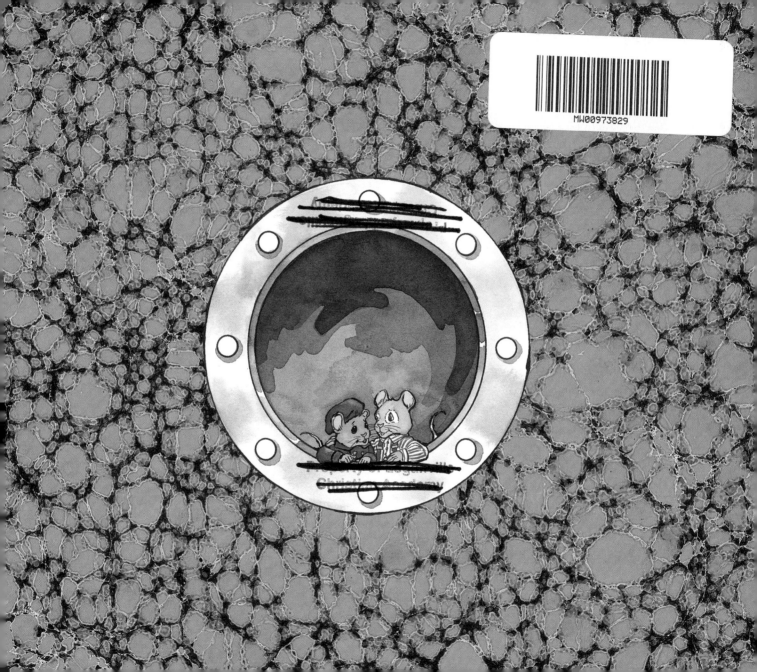

01-2401-799

THE *NEW!* CHRISTOPHER CHURCHMOUSE ADVENTURES

THE STOWAWAYS

Colossians 3:17 – "And whatsoever you do in word or deed, do all in the name of the Lord Jesus, giving thanks through Him to God the Father."

WRITTEN BY BARBARA DAVOLL
Pictures by Dennis Hockerman

MOODY

To our granddaughter, Emma Kathryn Walsh,
born February 9, 1998, to Tom and Lisa Davoll Walsh

"I have no greater joy
than to hear that my children walk in truth."
3 John: 4

MOODY PRESS CHICAGO © 1999 by BARBARA DAVOLL and DENNIS HOCKERMAN

All Scripture quotations, unless indicated, are taken from the *New American Standard Bible,* © 1960, 1962, 1963, 1968, 1971, 1972, 1973, 1975, 1977, and 1994 by The Lockman Foundation, La Habra, Calif. Used by permission.

Printed in the United States of America

Dear Diary,

When Papa and I went to meet the boat, Lukas, my cousin and I got left behind on the boat. We didn't get off in time. Papa and the rest of Lukas' family didn't know we got left. We don't know where the boat is going, but we're sailing somewhere. We will try hard to be brave.

Christopher

Christopher Churchmouse and his little cousin, Lukas, darted behind a pile of rope and slumped to the deck to catch their breath. The mice were exhausted from running around the big ocean liner, trying to hide.

"We'll rest here a few minutes, Lukas. I think it will be safe. The people can't see us back here," Christopher panted, taking in big gulps of air.

"What do now we do?" asked his cousin in his funny way of speaking. "I so want to come to America my heart crying. I am so miss for my family."

Christopher looked at him with sorrow in his eyes. "I know how you feel, Lukas. I miss my mama and papa, too. But we couldn't help getting stuck on this boat, could we?"

Lukas and his American cousin, Christopher, had been accidentally trapped on the ship when Lukas and his family arrived in America. The boat had sailed before the two mice could get off. He and Christopher had no idea where the boat was headed or when they would get home again.

Christopher leaned his head back against the wall. Looking up, suddenly he forgot how tired he was. "Look up there, Luke," he squeaked excitedly. He was pointing to a lifeboat that was hanging above the ship's rail. "I think I've found a place for us to hide."

Lukas stared at Christopher with his big eyes. "You be silly, Chris," he said with disgust. "We can no do. My family came over whole big ocean on this boat. We had better place to hide than up high in lifeboat."

"Well, where did you hide when you came over?"

"Not very good place," Lukas admitted sadly. "Dark and drippy. But no people to throw us overboard," he said, brightening up a bit. "I show you. It be down in the 'hole' of the ship. Come on!"

Lukas scampered away with Christopher following close behind him. Soon the cousins came to some steps and quickly skittered down them. When they reached the bottom, Lukas led Christopher to a wooden door and showed him how to squeeze under it. It was so dark inside that Chris could see nothing.

"Careful be! Is always slippery," warned Lukas.

"Phew! It smells in here," Christopher whispered. "How did your family stand it for your whole trip?"

"We do anything to be free, Cousin. We leave everything behind to come to your wonderful America. Come. I find our old mouse hole."

Just then a rough voice sneered, "Well, if it isn't sweet little Lukas that's come back to us! America not so great as you thought, Lukie? Or did you decide you want to go back home to the old country?"

"It's pirate rat," Lukas whispered. "Don't frightened be."

There was the sound of shuffling feet in the half darkness, and Chris knew that he was being looked over by the shifty-eyed gang of pirate rats. He admired the bravery of his cousin, who seemed to be unafraid of them.

"We no bother you, Blackie," said Lukas. "I find my friend in the kitchen – Pierre. He find us some food."

"No need for that, Lukas," simpered Black Whisker. "We have plenty of bread and cheese and some good wine. See!"

When he waved his paw, the gang of rats lit a candle, and there before them was food set up on some old bricks. Christopher was so hungry his mouth began to water, but Lukas put out a paw to stop him from going to the table.

"Then he said out loud, America be fine, Blackie." "My family be safe, and they be free. A little trouble I had getting off boat, that's all. This be my American cousin, Christopher Churchmouse. This be pirate rat—Black Whisker," he told Christopher.

Christopher's eyes were becoming accustomed to the darkness of the ship's hold, and he could see better now. Looking up, he saw the fearsome face of Black Whisker.

The pirate rat had a patch over one eye and a big scar across his nose where no fur grew. Long black whiskers hung down, and he was huge!

"H-How do you do, Mr. Black Whisker," the churchmouse said politely.

Black Whisker threw back his head and laughed a nasty laugh. "How do I do? As mean as I can," he sneered. "Hey, gang, we've got a little churchmouse boy with us! Come on over and meet him."

"Thank you, no, Blackie. We find food ourselves," Lukas said firmly.

"Oh, come on, my little friends. Look at the fine food and the wine Black Whisker and his gang enjoy. There are no finer wines than here in the wine cellar. Come! Drink and eat with us, and you can be a part of our gang."

But Lukas shook his head. "No, thank you, Blackie. You know my family not drink wine."

"Oh, that's right!" Blackie responded with a snarl. "So sorry I asked. I see now that your American cousin is a goody-goody *churchmouse* like the rest of your sniveling family. Of course, he wouldn't drink wine. And he wouldn't like our food either — since we steal it."

Christopher gasped. *These pirates steal their food! he thought. Oh, what would Papa and Mama think of that!* He was so glad that Lukas would not eat or drink with them.

"Please excuse, Black Whisker," said Lukas politely. "My friend in the kitchen be the chef's pet mouse. He will some scraps for us find. We go to our old mouse hole after we eat."

"Certainly," Blackie said, bowing in front of them in a mocking way. "If you prefer scraps to the excellent cheese and wine we enjoy. Please give my regards to the chef," he mocked, allowing the two little mice to pass by him.

Black Whisker and the gang of pirate rats silently watched the cousins as they quickly walked past. Just beyond the barrels of wine was a large door.

"Under here, Christopher," Lukas said as they came to the door. "This lead us to kitchen. Follow me." Squeezing under, they came to another stairway. Lukas led the way up the steps and into a big kitchen. It was here the chef prepared all the food for the people on the ship.

"Over here," Lukas said. Putting a paw to his lips, he signaled Christopher to be quiet.

Then Christopher saw a man in a white coat and chef's hat. He was standing in front of a stove, stirring something. Sitting on the counter beside the stove was a white mouse. The mouse was dressed in a tiny white coat and chef''s hat, just like the chef. Tiptoeing up behind the man, Lukas squeaked loudly.

The man whirled around in surprise. His big spoon clattered to the floor. "Can it be! Look, Pierre! Is this not our dear leetle friend Lukas?" he cried, bending over and picking up Lukas. "You come back to old Jacques [Jock]," he cried, stroking Lukas with his thumb. "And *another* little Lukas!" Then he gently picked up Christopher and began petting him.

As he said this, the pet mouse on the counter took off his hat and threw it in the air. "Now we can be jolly again," he cried. "Lukas is back! But why are you here, Lukas? Did you not like America?"

"We be trapped on the boat, Pierre," said Lukas sadly. "My mama and papa and little Narnie, they be free in America. My American cousin Christopher and I trapped on boat."

The chef seemed as glad to see the mice as was his pet mouse, Pierre. "My dear little mouse friends, welcome. But I am so sorry you are not with your family. They must be very sad — like old Jacques was when he thought you leave him, Lukas. But now we have another journey together. *Oui?*" he asked.

"*Oui* means 'yes' in French," Lukas explained to Christopher. "Jacques and Pierre are from France."

"It's very nice to meet you, Jacques and Pierre," Christopher said from his perch in Jacques's hand. He could tell right away that he would like this Frenchman and his mouse.

"We already meet up with Black Whisker," said Lukas to Pierre, who had jumped up into Jacques's hand also. "He offer us food and drink, but we say no."

"Indeed not!" Pierre responded. "Those rats are big problem for Jacques. They steal from kitchen and make big trouble. But you and little cousin will be fine. Old Jacques care for you on your way to our country, France! And now for the finest of French cuisine* [kwi-zeen] prepared by finest of French chef. *Oui?*"

"Exactly so!" answered Jacques. "Serve our friends the very best we have to offer them, Pierre!"

Suddenly things began to happen. Jacques put all the mice on the counter. In a whisker of time, Pierre had set a tiny round table with a white tablecloth, mouse-size candles, silver, and china. Jacques then placed on the dishes very small portions of the food he was preparing. It was a feast fit for a king.

"Now eat hearty, my little friends," Jacques said, rubbing his hands together happily. "This is your dining room. You will dine by candlelight tonight—not in the dark as the pirate rats do. Jacques and Pierre are your friends. We will have good time together on our way to France. *Oui?*" he asked delightedly.

"*Oui!*" Christopher and Lukas chorused. To think that they had been so frightened only a few hours before. They had seen no way out. Now they knew where they were going, and they had a wonderful friend to help them on their journey.

Christopher and Lukas sat enjoying their delicious meal while Pierre served them and Jacques returned to his cooking. Chewing thoughtfully, Christopher said to his cousin in his most grown-up voice, "I think I like French cuisine very much."

"*Oui, oui,*" Lukas answered, laughing and winking at Pierre.

This is going to be quite an adventure, Christopher thought. A French adventure, it seems.

THROUGH THE MOUSEHOLE

What an adventure Christopher and Lukas are having! – first, for them to be stranded on the boat and, then, to run into those fearful pirate rats.

And did you notice that Lukas had already made up his mind that he wouldn't drink the pirates' wine or eat their stolen food? It is always easier to resist Satan and not do bad things if we think about it beforehand. That way, we can make up our minds ahead of time that we won't sin.

Today there are a lot of temptations for kids. The Bible tells us we should never put things into our bodies that will harm us. That includes smoking, drinking, and using drugs. Those things are very bad for our bodies. The Lord Jesus wants us to say no to Satan when he tempts us.

I thought it was wonderful how the little mice were honored by Jacques and Pierre. They had a banquet prepared for them, didn't they? Do you know the Lord Jesus is preparing a banquet table in heaven for us if we belong to Him? We can say no to Satan a lot easier when we know what the Lord is preparing for us who love Him.

A great Bible verse to remember is Colossians 3:17. It says, "Whatever you do in word or deed, do all in the name of the Lord Jesus, giving thanks through Him to God the Father."

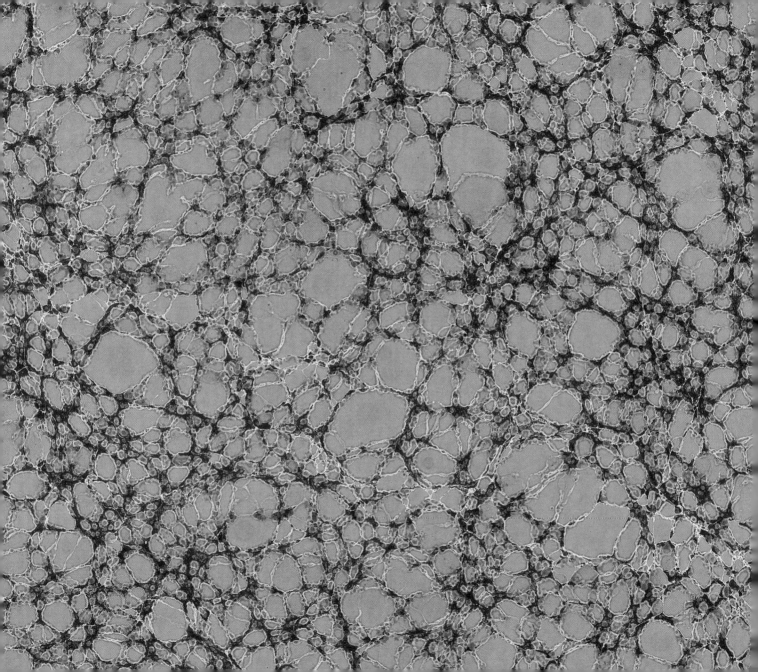